melville house classics

THE
DEATH
OF IVAN
ILYCH

THE DEATH OF IVAN ILYCH

LEO TOLSTOY

TRANSLATED BY IAN DREIBLATT

MELVILLE HOUSE PUBLISHING
BROOKLYN, NEW YORK

THE DEATH OF IVAN ILYCH WAS FIRST PUBLISHED IN RUSSIAN IN 1886.

TRANSLATION © IAN DREIBLATT 2008

SERIES DESIGN: DAVID KONOPKA

MELVILLE HOUSE PUBLISHING
145 PLYMOUTH STREET
BROOKLYN, NY 11201

WWW.MHPBOOKS.COM

ISBN 978-1-933633-54-1

FIRST MELVILLE HOUSE PRINTING: MAY 2008

LIBRARY OF CONGRESS CATALOGING-IN-PUBLICATION DATA

TOLSTOY, LEO, GRAF, 1828-1910.
  [SMERT' IVANA IL'ICHA. ENGLISH]
  THE DEATH OF IVAN ILYCH / BY LEO TOLSTOY ; TRANSLATION BY
IAN DREIBLATT.
    P. CM.
  ISBN 978-1-933633-54-1
  I. DREIBLATT, IAN, 1980- II. TITLE.
  PG3366.S6D74 2008
  891.73'3--DC22
                                    2008009409

PRINTED IN CANADA.

THE DEATH OF IVAN ILYCH

I   Within the edifice of the Public Courts, the advocates and prosecutor from the proceedings of the Melvinski trial spent a recess together in the office of Ivan Yegorovich Shebek, and a conversation arose about the details of the well-known Krasovski case. Fyodor Vasilyevich maintained heatedly that it was beyond their jurisdiction; Ivan Yegorovich insisted on the opposite; while Pyotr Ivanovich stayed out of the debate, lazing instead through the day's *Gazette*, which had just arrived.

"Gentlemen! It seems that Ivan Ilych has died."

"Is that so?"

"Here, read for yourself," he told Fyodor Vasilyevich, handing him the paper, its ink still damp.

Bordered in black were the words: *Praskovya Fedorovna Golovina with deepest sadness informs relatives and acquaintances of the passing of her beloved spouse, member of the Court of Justice, Ivan Ilych Golovin, on February 4th of this year, 1882. The funeral will be Friday at one o'clock in the afternoon.*

Ivan Ilych had been a colleague to all of the assembled men, and they had all liked him. He'd been ill for weeks with a disease said incurable. His post had been kept open for him, but rumors had swirled that in the event of his death Alekseyev might replace him, and either Vinnikov or Shtabel might then rise to replace Alekseyev. And so it was that each man in the office, on learning of the death of Ivan Ilych, thought first of what implications the death might hold for him, what reshufflings it might occasion for him and his colleagues.

Likely I'll be promoted to either Shtabel or Vinnikov's job, Fyodor Vasilyevich thought. *It's long been promised to me, and it'll mean an eight hundred ruble raise per year, not to mention a new office.*

Now I'll have to apply to have my wife's brother transferred from Kaluga, Pyotr Ivanovich thought. *She'll be so happy. She won't be able to complain anymore that I never do anything for her family.*

"I did suspect he'd never recover," Pyotr Ivanovich said aloud. "It's too bad."

"But what did he actually have?"

"The doctors couldn't say—or they could, but each said something different. When I last saw him I thought he'd recover."

"And I haven't been over to see him since before the holidays! I kept meaning to go."

"So, did he have any property?"

"I think his wife has a little bit—but really just a trifle."

"Well, we'll have to go out there. They lived awfully far away."

"You mean they lived awfully far away from you. Everything's far from you."

"He just can't ever let me off the hook for living across the river," Pyotr Ivanovich said, smiling to Shebek. And they discussed distances between places in the city, and went back to the courtroom.

Apart from the curiosity it gave them about the changes in office it might occasion, the very fact of the death of a close acquaintance awoke as ever in each of them a familiar gladness: it's *he* who's dead, not me.

Each of them either thought or felt, *Well, certainly, he's dead, but, after all,* I'm *not.* The close acquaintances, the so-called friends, of Ivan Ilych, could think only of the litany of banal obligations they'd have to meet, the funeral to endure, the visit to pay the widow.

Fyodor Vasilyevich and Pyotr Ivanovich were closer than the others.

Pyotr Ivanovich had been a friend since law school and considered himself in Ivan Ilych's debt.

Having told his wife at dinner the news of Ivan Ilych's death and the possibility of her brother being transferred to their circuit, Pyotr Ivanovich, ignoring his usual evening relaxation, threw on his coattails and headed to Ivan Ilych's house.

At the gateway to the house stood a carriage and two coachmen. Downstairs, the hallway leading in was cluttered by a hat rack and a coffin lid that had been polished and decorated with tassels and gold-cord. Two ladies in black were shedding their minks. One of them, Ivan Ilych's sister, was an acquaintance of his; with the other face he was unfamiliar. Pyotr Ivanovich's colleague, Shvarts, had been headed downstairs, but, catching sight of him from the top step, stopped and winked, as though to say, *Ivan Ilych left his affairs in a clumsy mess. You and I are a different sort.*

Shvarts's face with its British-style mustachios and the slender figure he cut in his coattails had, as ever, an elegant solemnity, and this solemnity, always at odds with his playful spirit, here was rather piquant. Or so it seemed to Pyotr Ivanovich.

Pyotr Ivanovich waved the ladies ahead of him and slowly followed them to the stairs. Shvarts waited in place, and Pyotr Ivanovich quickly realized: he wanted to try and figure out a good spot for their next whist game. The ladies headed upstairs to the widow, and Shvarts, his lips pressed together solemnly but with a playful look in his eyes, indicated by a twitch of his brow a room to his right where the body was.

Pyotr Ivanovich went in, as one always does, unsure of what to do. All he knew was that to cross oneself is never offensive. But as for whether he should bow while doing so, he had no idea, and so he decided on a moderate course of action: entering the room, he crossed himself and bent a little at the knee, while he quickly scanned the room as best the movements of his arms and head allowed. There were two young people, possibly relatives, one still in high school, on their way out. An old woman standing motionless. And a lady with strangely arched eyebrows telling her something in a whisper. A vigorous, resolute assistant deacon in a frock coat was reading something loudly and with an expression that made any disagreement impossible. The butler's assistant, Gerasim, stepped lightly in front of Pyotr Ivanovich and sprinkled something across the floor. Watching him, Pyotr Ivanovich became suddenly aware of the faintly perceptible smell of a decaying body. He'd seen Gerasim on his last visit here, acting as a nurse to Ivan Ilych, who had always especially liked him. Pyotr Ivanovich continued crossing himself and bowed slightly in the direction of the coffin, the preacher, and some icons on a table in the corner. After a while, when he realized he'd been making the sign of the cross for too long, he stopped and began looking at the corpse.

The dead man was lying, as dead men always lie, especially heavily, his deadened limbs forever sinking into the cushions, his head forever bowing on the pillow, and he was on display, as dead men are always put on display, with his waxen yellow forehead speckled with bald spots and his nose sticking up as though pressing into his upper lip. He had changed much and grown even thinner since Pyotr Ivanovich had last seen him, but, as always happens after death, his face had grown handsomer, more dignified—more distinguished, in short, than it had ever been in life. The expression on his face seemed to say that what had needed to be done had been done, and done right. Beside this his expression also seemed to hold a warning, a reproach to the living. This seemed out of place to Pyotr Ivanovich, or, at least, inapplicable to him. Suddenly uncomfortable, Pyotr Ivanovich abruptly crossed himself one more time and hurriedly—maybe too hurriedly for propriety's sake, he worried—headed back out of the room.

Shvarts was waiting for him in the hallway, legs in a wide stance, fiddling with his top hat behind his back. Just the sight of that proper, elegant man brought Pyotr Ivanovich all the refreshment he needed. He felt that Shvarts stood above all this and would never surrender to the morbidities of convention. One glance at him said it: the observance of Ivan Ilych's funeral couldn't possibly suffice to break his commitment to his evening plans—that is, that nothing would get in the way of his playing cards that night, keep him from opening a new pack while the footman placed four new candles around the table; there was no reason on earth why the funeral proceedings should stop them from enjoying their evening. He said as much, in a whisper, as Pyotr Ivanovich was walking past, suggesting that they meet up at Fyodor Vasilyevich's. But apparently Pyotr Ivanovich wasn't fated to play whist that evening. The widow Praskovya Federovna—a short, fat woman who, despite every effort to the contrary, had continued a steady sidewise expansion from top to bottom—emerged from her bedroom with some other ladies. She was dressed all in black, with a lace veil shadowing eyebrows arched in the same odd manner as the woman's by the coffin. She stopped with the others at the door to the room where her husband lay, and said, "The service will begin at once. Please come in."

Shvarts bowed vaguely, then stood still, not accepting and not declining this invitation. Praskovya Federovna, recognizing Pyotr Ivanovich, let out a heavy sigh, walked up to him, and took hold of his hand.

"I know you were a true friend to Ivan Ilych . . ." And she looked at him, waiting for a response in kind.

Pyotr Ivanovich knew that just as he had needed to cross himself earlier, here he needed to press her hand, and breathe haltingly, and say, *Believe it!* And so he did exactly that, receiving exactly the response he'd desired: he was touched, and she was touched.

"Come, before the service begins. I need to speak with you," the widow said. "Give me your hand."

Pyotr Ivanovich gave her his hand, and they headed for the interior rooms, passing Shvarts, who winked sadly to Pyotr Ivanovich, a communicative, playful wink that seemed to say, *That's it for whist! Don't be mad if we find someone else to play. We'll just cut you in if you get a chance to escape.*

Pyotr Ivanovich sighed still more sadly and profoundly, and Praskovya Federovna squeezed his hand in thanks. Entering the drawing room, upholstered in pink cretonne and lit by a milky lamp, they sat at a table, she on a low sofa and Pyotr Ivanovich on a hassock whose springs shuddered oddly under his weight. Praskovya Fedorovna wanted to warn him to find another seat, but found that this warning would be incongruous with her present state, and so decided against it. Sitting on this hassock, Pyotr Ivanovich remembered how Ivan Ilych had set this room up, and sought his advice concerning this same pink cretonne with its green leaves. As she had walked past the table to sit down (the whole room was crowded with furniture and bric-a-brac), the widow had caught her black shawl on one of its corners. Pyotr Ivanovich got up to detach it, and the springs of the hassock, freed of his tyrannical weight, bounced up and nudged him. The widow started unhooking it herself, and so Pyotr Ivanovich sat back down, quelling the rebellion of the hassock. But she couldn't quite manage it, and Pyotr Ivanovich rose again, freeing the hassock to rebel against him. It even creaked. When all this was over, Praskovya Fedorovna produced a cleanly laundered cambric handkerchief and began weeping. The episode with the shawl and his war against the hassock had cooled his emotions somewhat, and Pyotr Ivanovich just sat now, looking miserable. This was the plodding state of affairs that Sokolov, Ivan Ilych's butler, interrupted with the news that the gravesite Praskovya Fedorovna had requested would cost two hundred rubles. She stopped weeping and, turning to Pyotr Ivanovich with a put-upon look, said in French that things were very difficult for her. Pyotr Ivanovich gave a silent signal that he saw no room to doubt as much.

"Have a cigarette, please," she said to him in a voice at once magnanimous and decimated, and turned back to Sokolov and the question of the price of the grave. Lighting up, Pyotr Ivanovich heard her ask in great detail about various cemetery plots, and then issue very firm instructions about which grave to buy. Besides that, she gave some very specific instructions for the choir. And then Sokolov left.

"I do everything myself," she told Pyotr Ivanovich, pushing the albums on the table to one side; and then, noticing that his cigarette ash threatened the tabletop, she passed him an ashtray without delay and said, "I find it pretentious to say that my grief prevents me from taking care of practical matters. On the contrary, if anything can—I don't want to say console me—but if anything can take my mind off it, it's seeing to his affairs." She again produced her handkerchief, as though about to cry, but then suddenly seemed to grab hold of herself, and spoke much more easily:

"I have something to discuss with you."

Pyotr Ivanovich leaned forward, trying carefully to control the springs of the hassock, which groaned and shifted under him regardless.

"In his last days he suffered terribly."

"Did he?" Pyotr Ivanovich asked.

"Oh, it was awful! For the last few hours—not minutes, mind you, but hours—he cried out constantly. For days he shouted in anguish. It was intolerable. I do not even understand how I withstood it. You could hear him three doors down. Oh, what I've been through!"

"And was he really aware of his surroundings?" Pyotr Ivanovich asked.

"Yes," she whispered, "to the last minute. He bid us goodbye a quarter-hour before he died, and asked that we bring Volodya elsewhere."

The thought of such suffering in someone he'd known so well, first as a carefree little boy, then in school, and later as an adult and colleague, suddenly filled Pyotr Ivanovich with horror, despite even this woman's affectation, as well as his own, which it was unpleasant to notice. All at once he couldn't shake the image of that forehead, the nose pressing into the lip, and he was afraid for himself.

Three days of horrible suffering, followed by death. That could happen to me at any moment, he thought, and a true terror came over him. But then right away, without his quite knowing how, the more customary thought came to him that this had happened to Ivan Ilych and not to him, that this should not and could not happen to him; that, in fact, to think in this way gave power to gloom and depression, which, as Shvarts clearly demonstrated, one must not do. And so, having reasoned his way through all this, Pyotr Ivanovich was reassured enough to ask in detail about the death of Ivan Ilych, as though death were a kind of unusual, adventurous process, peculiar to Ivan Ilych, with no bearing on Pyotr Ivanovich himself.

After various details about the truly horrible sufferings Ivan Ilych had endured (which were presented to him solely in terms of their effects on Praskovya

Fedorovna's nerves), the widow apparently saw a need to get down to business.

"Oh, Pyotr Ivanovich, it's so difficult, so awfully difficult, how terrible, how terribly hard." She broke down crying again.

Pyotr Ivanovich sighed, and waited for her to blow her nose. When she had, he spoke again. "Believe me . . ." and again she began talking, and got to what was, apparently, her main concern. Her questions centered on how she might refer to the death of her husband in requesting a grant from the government. She couched her questions in terms of seeking his advice regarding her pension, but it was immediately apparent to him that she knew everything there was to know on the subject—certainly far more than he did—and what she actually wanted was to find a way of getting more money. Pyotr Ivanovich tried to think something up but couldn't, and after—as a courtesy—condemning the stinginess of the government, he concluded that getting more was impossible. She sighed loudly and began obviously working to get rid of him. He understood, put out his cigarette, stood up, pressed her hand, and headed out to the front room.

In the dining room, with its clock that Ivan Ilych had been so glad he had found in an antique shop, Pyotr Ivanovich met a priest and a few other acquaintances who had just arrived, and then caught sight of a pretty young woman with a familiar face—Ivan Ilych's daughter. She was all in black. Her waist, very slim, seemed even slimmer. She had a gloomy, stubborn, almost hostile

look about her. She bowed to Pyotr Ivanovich as though
he were to blame for something. Behind her stood a rich
young man with the same affronted look, an examining
magistrate, her fiancé, as he had heard. He bowed
mournfully to them and was about to head into the room
where the body was when from under the staircase the
figure of Ivan Ilych's schoolboy son appeared, with a
frightful resemblance to his father. This was the young
Ivan Ilych whom Pyotr Ivanovich remembered from
school. His eyes were tear-clouded and had the look
of thirteen- and fourteen-year-old boys who have dirty
thoughts. When he saw Pyotr Ivanovich he scowled
with a harsh, shameful uncertainty. Pyotr Ivanovich
nodded to him and rejoined the observers of the body.
A funeral—candles, moans, incense, tears, blubbering.
It was underway. Pyotr Ivanovich stood with a sour look
on his face, sinking into his legs. He did not look at
the corpse even once, did not give in to any negative
thoughts, and was among the first to leave. Nobody was
in the vestibule until Gerasim, the butler's assistant,
darted out from the dead man's room, and, rummaging
with his strong hands through all the coats, found Pyotr
Ivanovich's.

"Well, Gerasim, brother . . ." Pyotr Ivanovich said
to avoid being silent. "Isn't it a shame?"

"It's God's will. We'll all know it," Gerasim
answered, flashing his teeth, the orderly white teeth of a
peasant. Then he quickly opened the door of the coach,
called out to the driver, helped Pyotr Ivanovich to his

seat and leapt back to the porch, as though figuring out exactly what to do next.

The fresh air was a relief after the smell of the incense, and the corpse, and the carbolic acid.

"Where to?" the coachman asked.

"It's not late. Take me to Fyodor Vasilyevich's house."

And Pyotr Ivanovich went there, and found them right at the end of their first rubber—a perfect time to deal himself in.

II   In its details the life of Ivan Ilych was the most simple
and the most ordinary and the most horrible.

Ivan Ilych died at the age of forty-five as a member
of the Court of Justice. His father, an official in
Petersburg, had carved out through various ministries
and departments a career path of the sort that ends in an
imaginary position. Men in Petersburg hold positions like
that when they clearly can no longer function, but have
too much seniority and have demonstrated too much
loyalty to be dismissed; the solution is a fictional post but
with a very real salary of six to ten thousand rubles per
year, on which a man can live to a ripe old age.

Just such a man was the Privy Councilor Ilya
Yefimovich Golovin, a superfluous member of several
superfluous institutions.

Of the three sons he had, Ivan Ilych was the second. The eldest had followed in his father's footsteps, albeit through a different series of ministries, and was fast approaching the age when, as with his father, his inertia would metamorphose into a salary. The youngest son was a failure. He had made a wreck of himself and ended up having to take work on the railway. Both his father and his brothers, and even more so their wives, didn't dislike him so much as fail, various emergencies notwithstanding, to recollect his very existence. Their sister had married Baron Gref, a functionary in the exact mold of his father-in-law. Ivan Ilych was said to be the *phénix de la famille*, neither cold and arithmetical like his older brother nor as ruinously uncivilized as his younger. He was right in the middle—a smart, lively man, nice and proper. He and his younger brother had begun a legal education together; though his brother was kicked out in his fifth year, Ivan Ilych himself completed his studies in good standing. In school he was already just as he would be for the rest of his life: a person of talent, cheerfully kindhearted and sociable, but strict in fulfilling what he reckoned his duty to be, and he reckoned his duty to be whatever his superiors told him it was. He had been nobody's toady, neither as a boy nor later in adulthood, but from the youngest age he had been drawn, as a bird to the air, toward people in the upper echelons of society, adopting their affect and view of life, and maintaining friendships with many of them. All the preoccupations of childhood and youth dissipated from him without leaving a trace; he was given to lust, and to vanity—even, toward the end of school, to liberalism—but was protected by a strong inborn sense of moderation.

At law school he had done some things that earlier would have seemed repugnant to him, and been disgusted with himself; but later on, having noticed that people of the highest standing did the same sorts of things and didn't reckon them evil, he didn't reconcile himself to them morally so much as manage utterly to forget about them, and he wasn't troubled in the least by the memories of what had happened.

On finishing law school he qualified for a tenth-rank civil service job and, having received some money from his father for his uniform, Ivan Ilych ordered some clothes from Sharmer's haberdashery, hung a medallion on his watch-chain that said *respice finem*, took leave of his professor and the prince who funded the school, had dinner with his classmates at Donon's restaurant, and, with his fancy new valise, linens, uniform, shaving kit, toiletries, and plaid traveling rug—all ordered and bought at the best shops in town—left for the countryside, where a seat as special secretary to a provincial governor had been secured for him by his father.

On arriving Ivan Ilych immediately set up for himself just as easy and pleasant a lifestyle as he had enjoyed in school. He worked, making a career and at the same time having some good fun; once in a while he traveled out to the districts, where he treated higher-ups and lower-downs alike with dignity. He executed all his orders, which mostly concerned sectarian conflicts, with an exactness and incorruptible honesty of which he could not avoid feeling proud.

In official matters he was, despite his youth and inclination toward frivolous amusements, absolutely disciplined, formal, and even severe; but in society he was often playful and witty and always good-hearted, proper and *bon enfant*, as the governor and his wife—in whose house he was welcome as family—often said of him.

In the provinces he had an affair with a lady who threw herself at the elegant young lawyer; there was also a milliner; and there were rowdy nights spent drinking with visiting aides-de-camp and after-dinner visits to a certain far-off street; and there was a bit of obsequiousness to the governor and even his wife—but all this was gone about with such a ringing tone of decency that nothing too bad could be said of it. It could all be explained in a phrase from the French, *il faut que jeunesse se passé*. Everything was done by clean hands, in clean shirts, speaking French words, and, most importantly of all, in the very highest strata of society—that is, approved of by the people of highest standing.

That was how Ivan Ilych worked for five years, until orders came through for a transfer. New judicial institutions were established, and so new people were necessary.

Ivan Ilych became just such a new person.

The post of examining magistrate was offered to Ivan Ilych, and he accepted it even though it was in another province and would mean the loss of all his established connections in favor of new ones. Ivan Ilych's friends saw him off with a group photograph and the presentation of a silver cigarette case.

As an examining magistrate Ivan Ilych was just as *comme il faut*, as proper, as able to maintain his official responsibilities and private life separately from one another, as able to inspire general respect, as he had been in the governor's office. The new office was, for Ivan Ilych, far more interesting and rewarding than his previous post. In his last job it had been fun to stroll lightly in his Sharmer's uniform past the quivering, expectant line of petitioners and officials who envied him, straight into the boss's office, to sit with him over tea and cigarettes. But the people who had actually relied on him, answered to his whims, were few, mostly police officials and, when he was sent out on special assignment, sectarians. He had liked to deal cordially, almost collegially, with these people; he had relished giving them the sense that this man, who could easily bring them to ruin, preferred instead to speak as a friend, to deal plainly. But the truth was that such people had, in his last post, been very few. Now, on the other hand, as an examining magistrate, Ivan Ilych felt that everyone, everyone without exception, even the most self-satisfied people, *everyone* was under his thumb. All he needed to do was scribble a few words down on letterhead and this important, self-satisfied person would be led before him as a defendant or a witness, and if he did not want the man seated he would have to stand, stand before him and answer his questions. Ivan

Ilych never abused his new authority; on the contrary, he tried to soften it. But his awareness of his own power, and the possibility of softening it, imbued his new office with a crowning fascination and deep appeal. In the work itself—that is, in making his investigations—Ivan Ilych very quickly picked up the art of blinding himself to all considerations outside the legal details of a case, and reducing even the most intricate affairs to a bit of simple, prescribed paperwork that totally excluded his own viewpoint and, most importantly, conformed to all required formalities. It was a new kind of legal work. He was one of the first people to put the reforms of 1864 into practice.

Having come into a new town to fill the position of examining magistrate, Ivan Ilych made new acquaintances and connections, re-established himself and adopted a somewhat new manner. He put himself at some respectable distance from the affairs of the governor's office, chose the finest circle of rich jurists and noblemen to associate with, and adopted a tone of breezy discontent with government, a moderate, cosmopolitan liberalism. And so, not having in any way altered the elegance of his toilet, Ivan Ilych stopped shaving his face and offered his beard the freedom to grow where it wanted.

The life of Ivan Ilych developed pleasantly as he settled into his new city. The society there, among whom opposition to the governor was strong, was friendly and good; his salary was greater than before, and whist, which he began to play, brought him real pleasure. He played happily, thinking fast and very subtly, and, for this reason, nearly always winning.

After two years of work in his new city Ivan Ilych met the woman he would marry. Praskovya Fedorovna Mikhel was the most desirable, cleverest, most radiant girl of Ivan Ilych's social scene. Among other amusements and distractions from his work as an examining magistrate Ivan Ilych began a playful, easy flirtation with Praskovya Fedorovna.

Ivan Ilych, when he had been working for the governor, would often go out dancing; as an examining magistrate it was a rare exception. He danced as though only to prove it: *I may be an agent of the reforms, I may have reached the fifth rank, but when it comes to dancing, I'm better than you, and you should know it.* And so occasionally he would, at the close of an evening, dance with Praskovya Fedorovna, and it was mainly through these dances that he won her over. She fell in love with him. Ivan Ilych had no fixed matrimonial intentions, but when a girl fell for him he thought, *Well, there's really no sense in* not *getting married.*

Praskovya Fedorovna came from a good family and wasn't bad-looking; there was a little property. Ivan Ilych might have hoped for a more radiant match, but this one was good enough. He had a salary, and he hoped her property might bring in just as much. A good relationship; she was a sweet, and pretty, and totally dependable woman. To say that Ivan Ilych got married because he'd fallen in love with someone who shared his perspectives on life would be as wrong as saying that he got married because the people of his social circle approved the union. Ivan Ilych got married for both reasons: he did well by himself marrying a woman like Praskovya Fedorovna, and at the same time he did what high society found proper.

So Ivan Ilych got married.

The wedding itself and the beginning of married life, with its new sensuality, new furniture, new crockery, new linens, up until his wife became pregnant, went very well, so well that Ivan Ilych had started to think marriage not only wouldn't spoil but would even sweeten his easy, pleasant, happy life, as approved by society and regarded by himself as natural. But in the first few months of his wife's pregnancy something new emerged, something so unanticipated and nasty, so heavy and indecent, that it could never have been stopped, and there was no way out of it.

His wife, without any provocation that Ivan Ilych was aware of—*de gaité de coeur*, as he described it to himself—began to shatter the pleasant decorum of their lives: she became jealous of him for no reason, demanded his unshared attentions all the time, carped at everyone, made ugly, brutish scenes in public.

At first Ivan Ilych hoped to wriggle out of the awkwardness of his situation with that same lighthearted yet proper attitude that had served him so well in the past: he tried to ignore his wife's moods, to act as though life hadn't changed, he'd invite friends over for a party, or else he'd try to leave, to head to a club or to see a friend. But one day his wife began upbraiding him with such bile, and continued at it so vehemently every time he neglected a task she'd set for him, clearly having decided not to cool down until he fell into line—that is, by sitting home like her in gnawing, gloomy dullness—that he really panicked. He realized that married life—at least with his wife—did not necessarily promote pleasantness and decency in a life; in fact it might well amount to an assault on these things, and so fortifications were necessary. Ivan Ilych began assembling means to this end. His professional responsibilities were all he could use to impose his independence on Praskovya Fedorovna, and so Ivan Ilych began to use the duties of his office to fortify a wall protecting his independent world from the jaws of his marriage.

With the birth of the child, various attempts at feeding her, many of which failed, and with illnesses real and imagined of child and mother alike, in which Ivan Ilych's sympathy was demanded but of which he could understand nothing, the need to cordon off for himself a world beyond his family became more urgent still.

As his wife became more irritable and demanding, Ivan Ilych moved his life's center of gravity closer and closer to the office. As he grew to care more about work he became more ambitious than he had ever been.

Very soon, within a year of his marriage, Ivan Ilych realized that married life, though it offered some comforts, was in fact a weighty and complicated affair, and that to fulfill one's duty to it—that is, to lead a proper life approved of by society—one needs a certain kind of attitude, as one does in professional matters.

And so Ivan Ilych devised an attitude toward married life. All he needed from it were home-cooked meals, a wife to manage his house, a bed, and, most importantly, the external appearance of decency as decided by public opinion. Beyond that, he looked for good cheer and, if he found it, was very grateful; if he immediately met rebuff and vituperation he left for the walled-off world of his office, where life was pleasant.

Ivan Ilych was appreciated as a good bureaucrat and in three years was promoted to Associate Public Prosecutor. His new responsibilities, the importance of them, the ability to bring anyone to trial, put anyone in jail, the publicity his speeches got, and the success Ivan Ilych had in all of this: it all made his job more attractive to him.

More children came. His wife grew even angrier and more querulous, but the posture Ivan Ilych had taken toward domestic life made him almost impervious to querulousness.

After seven years of service in that city Ivan Ilych was transferred to another province as a Public Prosecutor. They moved, money got tight, and his wife didn't like the town they had moved to. Admittedly, his salary was higher, but life was more expensive there; beside that, two of his children died, which did nothing to improve family life for Ivan Ilych.

Praskovya Fedorovna blamed her husband for everything that went wrong in their new home. Most conversations between husband and wife—especially if they concerned the children's education—led to matters that threatened to start old fights up again. There were still occasional stirrings of affection, but they didn't last long; they were like islets where the couple might anchor for a while, knowing they'd nonetheless have to set out again on a sea of veiled enmity that was expressed in their alienation from each other. This alienation might have bothered Ivan Ilych had he considered it wrong, but by now he regarded it not only as a healthy state of affairs, but as the goal of all family activities. His aim was to free himself more and more from these unpleasantnesses and to give them a semblance of harmlessness and decency; he accomplished this by spending less and less time with his family, and, when he had to, by strengthening his position through the inclusion of guests. But most important of all was that Ivan Ilych had his work. He concentrated all his worldly attention in his professional life. It absorbed him. The sense of his own authority, the ability to destroy anyone he wanted, his importance, even seen externally, in his swaggering into the courthouse or into meetings with subordinates, his success before superiors and inferiors, and, most of all, the mastery he felt over the cases he dealt with—all this gratified him, and together with the conversations he had with his colleagues, over meals or playing whist, filled his life. So all in all the life of Ivan Ilych was going as he thought it should go: pleasantly and properly.

He lived seven more years like this. His eldest daughter turned sixteen, another child died, and there was one son left, a little schoolboy who was the subject of a struggle. Ivan Ilych wanted him to go to law school, but Praskovya Fedorovna out of spite enrolled him in a high school. Their daughter had been taught at home and had turned out well; the boy wasn't slow either.

III   So went Ivan Ilych's life for seventeen years of marriage. He was already an established prosecutor who had turned down several possible transfers, holding out for a still more desirable post, when an unexpected and unpleasant circumstance shattered the calm of his life. Ivan Ilych had been expecting an appointment as presiding judge in a university city when suddenly Goppe stole a march on him and got the appointment. Ivan Ilych got grumpy about it, became reproachful, and quarreled with Goppe and his immediate superiors. Their relationships iced over and the next time he was skipped over again.

It was 1880, the most trying year of Ivan Ilych's life. It became clear that, on the one hand, his salary did not suffice for his lifestyle, while, on the other, he had been totally forgotten, which, though it seemed to him an immense, brutal injustice, everyone else took for business as usual. Not even his father had felt bound to help him. Everyone, he felt, had abandoned him, thinking his thirty-five hundred ruble salary completely normal, even lucky. He alone knew that with the injustices he had suffered, the eternal nagging of his wife, and the debts he'd been racking up by living beyond his means—he alone knew that his position was far from normal.

To save money that summer he filed for a leave of absence and went with Praskovya Fedorovna to stay with her brother in the country.

In the country with no professional life, Ivan Ilych felt for the first time not just ennui but a deep, intolerable melancholy, an existential boredom that convinced him life was impossible as he had been living it and drastic measures would have to be taken.

After a sleepless night pacing the terrace, he decided to go to Petersburg to secure for himself a transfer to another ministry, and to punish those who hadn't held him in high enough esteem.

Within a day, over the protests of his wife and brother-in-law, he had left for Petersburg.

He was going for one reason: to demand a position salaried at five thousand rubles a year. He did not have in mind any particular ministry, direction, or sort of work. All he needed was a job, a job for five thousand, in administration, in banking, on the railways, in one of the Empress Maria's Institutions, even in customs—

but the five thousand rubles was unnegotiable and so was a transfer out of the ministry that had failed to appreciate him.

And this is where Ivan Ilych's trip flowered into a surprising success. In Kursk, an acquaintance of his, F.S. Ilin, sat down beside him in the first-class carriage and described a telegram just received by the governor, to the effect that a change was being made in the ministry: Ivan Semyonovich would be acceding to Pyotr Ivanovich's seat.

The proposed change, aside from its meaning for Russia, had a special meaning for Ivan Ilych. If Pyotr Petrovich was being put forward, so too must be his friend Zakhar Ivanovich, and that augured terrifically for Ivan Ilych: Zakhar Ivanovich was a colleague and friend of his as well.

The news was confirmed in Moscow. And when he arrived in Petersburg, Ivan Ilych sought out Zakhar Ivanovich and secured a promise that he be returned to his old position at the Ministry of Justice.

After a week he sent a telegram to his wife:

Zakhar in Miller's place. On first report I receive appointment.

Thanks to this personnel change Ivan Ilych was unexpectedly appointed to a spot in his old ministry two ranks above his former colleagues, with a salary of five thousand rubles plus thirty-five hundred for relocation expenses. His animus against his enemies and the ministry shrank and vanished; Ivan Ilych was completely happy.

Ivan Ilych returned to the country in better cheer than he'd been in for some time. Praskovya Fedorovna had also lightened up, and they made a truce. Ivan Ilych recounted how they'd toasted him in Petersburg, how every one of his enemies had been disgraced, how they prostrated themselves now before him, how he was envied for his position, and especially how fiercely well-liked he was in Petersburg.

Praskovya Fedorovna listened attentively and acted convinced, never contradicting anything he said, centering all her plans on life in their new city. And Ivan Ilych was glad to see that these plans were his own, that they were on the same page, and that his life, having stumbled, would regain its customary character of pleasantness and decency.

Ivan Ilych had only come back to the country for a little while. He needed to return to the city to take up his new duties on September 10th and, beside that, needed time to settle into his new place, to move everything over from the province, and there was still much to buy and order; in short, to settle into just the life he had set his mind on, which was almost identical to the one Praskovya Fedorovna had set her heart on.

Now that everything had worked out so happily, with he and his wife agreeing on a goal and, beside that, hardly seeing each other, they were getting along better than they had since their first years of marriage. Ivan Ilych had thought to take his family with him right away, but his wife's sister and brother-in-law, who had suddenly become especially affectionate to his whole family, wouldn't hear of it, and so he set out alone.

Ivan Ilych set out, and the good spirits brought on by his success and marital concord, the one strengthening the other, did not desert him. A charming house turned up, just what husband and wife had been dreaming of. Accommodating, high-ceilinged reception rooms in the old style, a grand study well-placed, rooms for his wife and daughter, a little classroom for his son—the place might as well have been custom-designed for them. Ivan Ilych took on the decoration himself, chose wallpaper, bought more furniture, especially antiques he felt more *comme il faut*, oversaw the upholstering, and everything grew and grew toward the ideal he had set for himself. With things only half done, his expectations were already being exceeded. He understood how *comme il faut* it would be, how graceful and free of vulgarity, when everything was ready. As he drifted off to sleep at night he imagined how the reception room would look. Surveying the yet unfinished drawing room, he could already make out a fireplace, and a screen, an *étagère*, the little chairs scattered around, the dishes and plates on the walls, and the bronzes, all where they'd eventually be. He was pleased to think how it would overwhelm his Pasha and Lizanka, who shared his taste in decoration. They were expecting nothing even close to this. He had had especially good luck finding and getting bargains on antiques, which gave the place an especially aristocratic feel. He wrote letters describing the place as mediocre to build up their surprise. All this kept him so busy that not even his new job, which he had so looked forward to, was much more than a distraction from it. In court he had moments of absentmindedness: what kind of cornices to get for his curtains, straight or curved? He was so preoccupied that he often tinkered around himself, rearranging the furniture, rehanging the curtains. Once he had gotten onto a ladder to show the uncomprehending upholsterer how he wanted the drapes hung, and he had stumbled and nearly fallen, but being a strong and nimble man managed to catch himself and merely knocked his side on a knob on the window frame. The bruise was painful, but it healed quickly—Ivan Ilych felt especially cheerful and healthy for this whole period. He wrote, *I feel that fifteen years have been taken off my head*. He had thought he would finish by September, but everything dragged on until mid-October. Still, the results were charming, and not just to him—everyone said so.

In fact it was all exactly what you so often see among people who are not quite rich but want to seem as though they are, and so end up resembling only each other: damasks, ebony, flowers, carpets, and bronzes. Dark and shining—everything that people of a certain class use to resemble other people of the same class. And in his case the resemblance was so strong that the house was nearly impossible to distinguish from any other; but to him it all seemed somehow special. After meeting his family at the rail station he brought them into the polished readiness of the house, where a footman in a white tie opened a door into the flower-lined hallway, and later they went into the drawing room and study, gasping with pleasure. He was very happy, drove them everywhere, got drunk on their praise, and glowed from pleasure. At tea that evening Praskovya Fedorovna asked him, among other things, about his fall, and he broke out laughing and acted out the whole scene for them; his sudden flight had terrified the poor upholsterer.

"Good thing I'm so agile. Someone else might've been killed, and I just have a little bruise here. It hurts when you touch it, but it's already healing up. It's nothing."

And so they began living in their new home, which they realized, as one always does, after getting good and cozy, was just one room too small; and they grew accustomed to the new salary, which was inadequate by just a little, maybe five hundred rubles; still, life was very good. Things went especially well at first, before the place was completely set up, while work still needed to be done: buy this, order that, rearrange, adjust. Although there were occasional disagreements between husband and wife, both were so happy and had so much going on that everything resolved itself without a serious row. When they ran out of decorations to arrange, things got a little boring and seemed to lack something, but by then acquaintances had already been made and habits set, and life felt complete.

Ivan Ilych would spend his mornings in court and be back for dinner, and at first his mood would be good, although he suffered occasional vicarious indignities on behalf of the house (any spot on a tablecloth or the upholstery, any fray in the tassels of the window-blinds, drove him crazy: he had put so much work into the décor that any imperfection caused him pain). But in general Ivan Ilych's life was going just how he thought it should: easily, pleasantly, and properly. He woke up at nine, drank his coffee, read the paper, and then put on his uniform and headed to the court. There he slid right into his usual harness and got to dealing with petitioners, questions for the office, the office itself, court sessions both public and administrative. In all this it was necessary to block out everything that could be felt in the blood, since any vivacity always derails the administrative process; it was imperative to admit no relationship to anybody but an official one, and even then only on official terms. For example, if a man showed up wanting some information from Ivan Ilych, and that information didn't fall in his bailiwick, then Ivan Ilych would have absolutely nothing to say to him; but if the man did have some official business for him, the kind that can go on official stationery under a letterhead, Ivan Ilych would behave resolutely, doing everything in his power to help, observing the basic rules of friendly human interaction—which is to say he was courteous. But as soon as the official relationship expired, everything else evaporated, too. Ivan Ilych had practiced this skill for keeping his professional life discrete from his actual life for a long time, and had developed it to such a degree that he sometimes, like a virtuoso, would blend his personal and professional attitudes together, as though for fun. He allowed himself to do it because he felt sure he'd be able to disentangle them when he needed to, accentuating the official attitude, casting off the human. Ivan Ilych's cases went not just easily, pleasantly, and properly, but in fact virtuosically. Between sessions he smoked, drank tea, and chatted—a little about politics, a little on common topics, a little about cards, but most of all about professional appointments. And tired, but with the feeling of being a virtuoso—maybe a first violin—who has played a perfect concert, he would head home. At home his daughter and wife would have gone somewhere or else someone would be over; his son was in high school and would be preparing for tomorrow's classes with a tutor, poring over whatever it is that high schools teach. Everything was going well. After dinner, if there were no guests, Ivan Ilych would sometimes read whatever book everyone had been talking about, and in the evening sit down to business—that is, read through his files—comparing witnesses' depositions and noting which section of the legal code applied to them. He was neither bored nor enthralled by it. It was always boring when he knew there was a whist game going on somewhere; but when he didn't, it was better than sitting around alone or with his wife. Ivan Ilych's chief pleasures were little dinner parties he would throw for men and women of high social standing, and these were as much like other dinner parties as his drawing room was like other drawing rooms.

Once they had even given a dance. And Ivan Ilych had been very happy, and everything had been just right, except that he had a huge argument with his wife over pastries and sweets: Praskovya Fedorovna had made arrangements, but Ivan Ilych had insisted on getting everything from a pricey confectioner and he had bought too many pies, so the bill came to forty-five rubles and they had too many left over. The quarrel was nasty, and Praskovya Fedorovna chastised him: "You fool, you imbecile." He clutched at his head and heart and threatened divorce. But the evening itself had been enjoyable. The finest people were there, and Ivan Ilych danced with Princess Trufonova, sister of a woman famous for founding the Bear Ye My Burden Society. Professional pleasure was the pleasure of self-love; social pleasure was the pleasure of vanity; but Ivan Ilych's present pleasure was the pleasure of whist. He openly admitted that, at the end of the day, whatever sadness came to his life, the one pleasure that shone like a candle burning brightly above all else was whist: to sit down with good players, not novices but real partners and opponents, and especially to play four-handed (five-handed is annoying, because you have to sit a round out, though of course everyone pretends they don't mind at all), to have an intelligent, serious game (when the cards allow it), and later to have supper and drink a glass of wine. And after whist, especially after a small winning (a big one is unbecoming), Ivan Ilych would lay down to sleep in an especially good mood.

And so they lived. They moved in the very best social circles, and took visits from important people, and young people on their way up.

In the eyes of their social circle, man, wife, and daughter were in complete agreement and, by an unspoken compact, shook themselves free of the various friends and relatives who streamed fawningly into the drawing room with Japanese dishes on its walls. Soon these sycophants had ceased coming by, and only the very best of society was seen at the Golovin's. Young men came to court Lizanka, and Petrishchev, an examining magistrate and the son and sole heir of Dmitri Ivanovich Petrishchev, began paying her so much attention that Ivan Ilych wondered aloud to Praskovya Fedorovna: "Should we arrange a troika ride for them? Or some kind of performance?" That was how they lived. And everything kept up like that, nothing changing, and it was all going terribly well.

IV   They were all in good health. Ivan Ilych sometimes complained of a funny taste in his mouth or a sort of dull discomfort in the left side of his belly, but you could hardly call it a malady.

Still, over time the discomfort—not quite a pain—began to grow into a strange feeling of pressure in his left side and a general sort of malaise. Ever stronger and stronger, it started to mar the pleasantness of the easy, proper life the Golovin family had settled into. Husband and wife began quarreling ever more constantly, and soon the ease and pleasantness of their lives dissipated, and maintaining proper appearances became a chore. They began making scenes again. The sea was again spotted with islets—and few of them—where husband and wife could get together without exploding at each other.

And Praskovya Federovna, not without justification now, declared her husband's character heavy and difficult. With characteristic exaggeration she even said that he had always been beastly, that surviving twenty years of it had squeezed the resources of her goodness to the last. It was true that he now started their fights. He would always raise his quibbles just before dinner, as he started into his soup. He might find some imperfection in the china, or that the food wasn't done right, his son had his elbows on the table, he didn't like his daughter's hairstyle. And whatever it was, he blamed Praskovya Fedorovna. At first she had objected and volleyed the nastiness right back at him, but once or twice he had raged so rabidly at the beginning of dinner that she realized it was some physical derangement brought on by eating, and grew resigned; she stopped objecting, and decided just to rush everyone through meals. By her acquiescence Praskovya Fedorovna did herself great credit. But having decided that her husband had a fierce temper and had made her life unhappy, she began pitying herself—and the more she did, the more she despised her husband. She was at the point of wishing he would die, if never quite sincerely: after all, it would mean the end of his pittance of a salary. This pitted her even more strongly against him. If even his death couldn't save her, she must be experiencing the most dreadful kind of unhappiness; she was irritated, but concealed it, and her hidden irritation gave strength to his irritation.

After one scene in which Ivan Ilych had been particularly unjustified, and after which he had said by way of excuse that he was certainly irritable but it was because he did not feel well, she told him that if he was sick he needed treatment, and she demanded that he visit a well-known doctor.

So he went. Everything was just as he had expected; everything was done just as it always is. The doctor's pretentious self-importance was familiar—he had seen the same in himself at court—and the sounding, and listening, the needless questions with obvious answers, and a heavy look that seemed to say, *Listen, just leave it to us, we'll take care of everything—we know precisely how to make the arrangements, it's the same for anybody.* It was exactly the same as at court. This famous doctor cut exactly the same figure to Ivan Ilych that he himself must have cut presiding before the accused.

The doctor said: "This-and-that and such-and-such indicate an et-cetera-and-so-forth inside of you; but if my investigations don't confirm blah-blah-blah and you-get-the-idea, we'll have to assume so on and so forth. And if we assume that . . ." and so on. Just one question mattered to Ivan Ilych: was his condition serious, or not? But the doctor ignored this mislaid curiosity. From his point of view, it seemed idle and not up for discussion; his diagnosis was a toss-up between a floating kidney, chronic catarrh, and appendicitis. It wasn't a question of the life or death of Ivan Ilych, but a quarrel between his floating kidney and appendix. And the doctor settled it—brilliantly, it seemed to Ivan Ilych—in favor of the appendix, with the proviso that his urine sample might shed new light on things that would require a reconsideration of the case. The doctor accomplished this all with the same brilliance that Ivan Ilych himself had displayed thousands of times for the defendants who had stood before him. It was with just that brilliance that the doctor triumphantly, even exultantly, made his diagnosis, looking down his glasses at the accused. From his summary Ivan Ilych drew the conclusion that things were bad. That is, it was bad for *him*; as for the doctor and everyone else, well, it didn't matter much. The realization hit Ivan Ilych hard, calling forth a great tide of self-pity, and great fury at a doctor who could be indifferent to matters of such importance.

But he did not say anything; he stood up, laid some money on the table, and, after letting out a sigh, spoke:

"I suppose patients like me often put uncomfortable questions to you," he said. "In general, is this a dangerous illness or not?"

The doctor glared at him through his glasses with one eye, as if to say: *If the accused will not confine himself to the questions put to him, I shall be obliged to have you removed from this hall of justice.*

"I have already told you what I consider necessary and expedient," the doctor said. "Further testing will complete my diagnosis." And the doctor bowed.

Ivan Ilych left slowly, climbed disconsolately into his coach, and went home. The whole way he racked his brain over everything the doctor had said, trying to translate all the muddy scientific jargon into simple language and find in it an answer to the question *Is it bad, is it really something very bad, or is it nothing to worry about?* And it seemed to him that the gist of everything the doctor had said was that things were very bad indeed. Everything Ivan Ilych rode past seemed clothed in sadness. The coachmen sad, and the houses, the passersby, the shops also seemed sad. And that ache, that dull, rueful, ache that would not relent for a second seemed, combined with every unclear word the doctor had said, to take on still heavier implications. Ivan Ilych now regarded it closely, with a new feeling of gravity.

When he got home he began telling his wife the story. At first she listened, but in the middle of the report their daughter walked in with a hat on: she was planning on going for a ride with her mother. With an effort she forced herself to sit down and make herself a party to the tedium, but she couldn't be still for long, and so her mother was unable to hear the whole thing.

"Well, I'm very glad," his wife said. "Now listen, just make sure you take your medicine, and watch the dosages. Here, give me the prescription, I'll send Gerasim to the pharmacist's." And she went to get dressed.

With her in the room he had barely been able to take a breath, and with her gone he let out a heavy sigh.

"Well, who knows," he said. "Maybe it really is nothing after all."

He started taking his medicine, following the doctor's instructions (which had changed on examination of his urine). But as it happens, some confusion arose, some disparities between the treatment he was supposed to follow and the results he was supposed to expect. The doctor couldn't be reached, and things weren't turning out as the doctor had told him they would. He must have forgotten, or else lied, or else been hiding something.

But all the same Ivan Ilych followed his instructions exactly, and there was at first some consolation in knowing what to do.

After his visit to the doctor, Ivan Ilych devoted most of his time to following the doctor's orders about hygiene and medicine precisely, and to closely observing his pain and everything that came out of his body. His main interests in life became other people's sickness and other people's health. When people around him would talk about someone who was sick, about someone who had died, about someone who had made a recovery, and especially about an illness like his own, his ears would perk up and, trying to hide his agitation, he would ask numerous questions and apply the answers to himself.

The pain did not let up, but Ivan Ilych tried to convince himself he was feeling better. And he could fool himself, if there was nothing making him edgy. But as soon as he had a spat with his wife, or a bad day at work, lousy luck at whist, anything, he would immediately feel the full force of his ailment; in the past he had dealt with these setbacks: *I'll make up for it, I'll prevail, wait this out, get a grand slam*. Now the slightest misfortune overcame him and plunged him into despair. He would tell himself, *Here I've just begun my recovery, the medicine finally kicking in, and now all these damned setbacks, this lousy luck . . .* And he cursed the events and the people who had made trouble for him and were killing him, and he felt that his rage might be killing him too; but he couldn't help it. It would seem—one would think—that he should have realized that the fulminations he poured on the circumstances and people in his life were making his condition worse, and that for this reason he should pay less attention to all the negative things that happened. But he explained it to himself in just the opposite way: telling himself that what he needed was peace and quiet, he went after everything that shattered that peace, and that quiet, and at even the tiniest irritation he became enraged. His condition was worsened by everything he read in medical books and all the advice he got from doctors. He was getting worse so gradually that he could trick himself, comparing one day with another—there was never much change from day to day. But when he consulted with doctors it seemed to him that he was going downhill fast. Despite that, he consulted with doctors constantly.

This month he had visited another famous one, and this one told him almost exactly what the first one had, but put the questions differently. And consulting with this eminence of the medical establishment only aggravated Ivan Ilych's doubts and fears. A friend of a friend of his—a very good doctor—diagnosed him with a totally different illness and even though he promised he would recover, his questions and assumptions confused Ivan Ilych even more deeply and made his doubts worse. Another doctor—a homeopath—offered yet another diagnosis and gave him a new prescription, which Ivan

Ilych, concealing it from everyone, took for a week. But after a week, feeling no better, he had lost trust in all the medications he was taking, and fell into an even deeper despondency. One time a lady of his acquaintance told him about the healing power of icons. Ivan Ilych found himself listening closely to her and even toying with the idea that this might make sense. But then he became alarmed at himself. *Have I really gone so soft?* he asked himself. *What mumbo-jumbo! It's all nonsense, I can't give in to superstition. Having chosen a doctor, I should follow his treatment. So that's what I'll do. It ends now. I won't think about it, I'll keep strictly to the doctor's treatment plan until summer. And then it'll be clear. For now I've got to stop wavering!* It was easy to say, but impossible to follow through with. The pain in his side tormented him constantly, even seemed to be getting worse, becoming incessant, while the taste in his mouth got constantly stranger. His breath seemed to have taken on a revolting smell, and he lost his appetite and became very feeble. He couldn't fool himself: something terrifying, new, and more significant than anything else that had ever happened in his life was happening within him. And only he himself understood it, the world neither could nor wanted to, and everyone behaved as if everything was exactly as it had been before. That tormented Ivan Ilych worst of all. Even at home, he saw that his wife and daughter, their social lives in full swing, understood nothing, and were annoyed that he was so gloomy and demanding, as though it were his fault. Although they tried to hide it, he saw he was an albatross to them, and that his wife had come up with a special policy for dealing with his illness no matter what he said or did. It went like this:

"You know," she told her friends, "Ivan Ilych cannot follow his doctor's orders strictly like a normal person. One day he'll take his drops, stick to his diet, get to bed at a decent hour; then suddenly, the next, if I'm not paying attention, he forgets his drops, eats sturgeon even though the doctor forbids it, and sits around playing whist till one in the morning."

"Oh, come on, when was that?" Ivan Ilych said with annoyance. "Maybe once, at Pyotr Ivanovich's."

"And yesterday with Shebek."

"It didn't make any difference—I was in too much pain to sleep."

"Oh, whatever the reason is, that way you'll never get better and just go on torturing us."

In short, Praskovya Fedorovna's policy toward the illness of her husband, which she elaborated to him as well as to anyone else who would listen, was that it was all Ivan Ilych's fault, just one more stone he was piling atop his wife. Ivan Ilych had the feeling this escaped her lips involuntarily, but that made it no easier for him to hear.

In court Ivan Ilych began noticing—or thought he'd noticed—the same strange attitude toward him: people seemed to be keeping a close eye on him, as though his position might soon be vacated. Then his friends started teasing him gently for his suspicions, as though the horrible and terrifying thing that was happening inexplicably inside him without warning, eating unendingly at him and irresistibly dragging him off, were the funniest thing in the world. Shvarts especially upset him, with the playfulness, vitality, and *comme il faut* demeanor that reminded Ivan Ilych of himself ten years younger.

Friends came over to play cards, sat down around the table. They dealt, bending the new cards to break them in, he sorted the diamonds in his hand; he held seven. His partner said *No trumps* and supported him with two diamonds. What more could he want? It should have been lively, good fun—they had a grand slam. But suddenly Ivan Ilych felt that gnawing pain, the taste in his mouth, and it seemed savage to be so happy about a grand slam in whist.

He looks at his partner Mikhail Mikhailovich, who is tapping on the table with a sanguine hand, and politely, indulgently, pushing the tricks to Ivan Ilych rather than grab them himself, as though to give him the pleasure of collecting them while sparing him the trouble of stretching his arm out. *What does he think, that I'm so weak I can't reach out that far?* Ivan Ilych thinks and, forgetting what he is doing he trumps his own partner, missing the grand slam by three tricks. And it is awful to see how upset Mikhail Mikhailovich is, while he himself doesn't care in the least. And most dreadful of all is to think about *why* he doesn't care.

Everyone sees what a hard time he is having, and they tell him, "We can stop, if you're tired. You need to rest up." Rest up? No, he's not tired in the least, they'll finish the rubber. Everyone is gloomy and silent. Ivan Ilych feels that he has cast upon them a gloom he cannot get to dissipate. They eat supper and go their separate ways, and Ivan Ilych is left alone with the awareness that his life is poisoned and is poisoning the lives of others, and this poison doesn't grow weaker, but rather gets stronger and stronger in the pit of his being.

And in the pain of this realization, not to mention his physical pain, not to mention his horror, he had to lie down in bed, often to be kept awake by the ache of it all for the better part of the night. And the next morning he would have to get up, get dressed, go to court, talk, write, or, if he didn't go, stay home for twenty-four hours of which every single one was raw torture. To live like that, on the very edge of death, was all he could do, without a single person who could understand or feel sympathy for him.

V   A month or two went by like that. His brother-in-law came to town to stay with them a week before the New Year. Ivan Ilych had been in court. Praskovya Fedorovna has gone out for groceries. Stepping into his study at home, he found his brother-in-law, a healthy, ruddy man, unpacking his suitcase. When he heard Ivan Ilych come in he lifted his head and looked at him for a second in silence. The look he gave revealed everything to Ivan Ilych. His brother-in-law had opened his mouth to gasp, and then caught hold of himself. In that small gesture, everything was confirmed.

"I guess I've changed?"

"Yes . . . a little bit."

And after that, no matter how Ivan Ilych tried to return the conversation to the question of how he looked, his brother-in-law wouldn't say anything. Praskovya Fedorovna came home and her brother went in to see her. Ivan Ilych locked the door behind him and began checking himself in the mirror—first head-on, then in profile. He grabbed a portrait of himself with his wife and compared it with what he saw in the mirror now. The change had been immense. Then he rolled his sleeves up to the elbow, looked at his arms, sat down on the ottoman, and fell into a mood blacker than night.

Don't, don't, he told himself, and sprang to his feet, walked to the table, opened a case file, tried to read it but couldn't. He unlocked the door, went into the hall. The door to the drawing room had been shut. He tiptoed up to it and started eavesdropping.

"No, you're exaggerating," Praskovya Federovna was saying.

"Exaggerating how? You can't see it—he's a dead man. Look into his eyes. There's no light in them. What has he actually got?"

"Nobody knows. Nikolayev—" that was another doctor "—said something, but I don't know. Leshchetitsky—" that was the famous one "—said the opposite..."

Ivan Ilych walked away, went into his room, laid down and began to think: *a kidney, a wandering kidney.* He thought back on everything the doctors had told him, how it had come loose, and how it now wandered. By the strength of his imagination he tried to catch that kidney and hold it still, to give it strength; so little was needed, it seemed to him. *No, I'll go to Pyotr Ivanovich's* (the friend who had recommended the doctor). He rang, ordered the carriage, and got ready to go.

"Where are you going, Jean?" his wife asked with an especially sad and unusually kind look on her face.

Her unaccustomed tenderness angered him. He shot her a morbid glance.

"I need to go to Pyotr Ivanovich's."

So he headed off to see Pyotr Ivanovich, and together they went to see his friend the doctor. He was in, and they chatted for a long time.

Going over the anatomic and physiological details of what the doctor thought was going on in him, Ivan Ilych understood everything.

It was one little thing, just the smallest thing wrong, in his appendix. He could recover from all this. Just strengthen one organ, and check on the activity of another, absorption would occur, and everything would right itself.

He was a little late for dinner. He ate, talking cheerfully, but it took a long time before he was able to force himself back to his room to work. Finally he went to his study and immediately sat down at the desk. He read through files, trying to get something accomplished, but couldn't shake the awareness that he'd put off an important matter that held his heart in it, which he would get back to as soon as he finished. When he was done he remembered where his heart was—in his appendix. But he refused to give himself over to it, and headed into the drawing room for tea. Guests were over, talking and playing the piano and singing; the examining magistrate who was his daughter's intended was there. Ivan Ilych spent the evening, as Praskovya Fedorovna remarked, more happily than usual, but he didn't forget for a second that he had put off important thoughts of his appendix. At eleven o'clock he excused himself and headed to his bedroom. Since falling ill he had been sleeping alone, in a small guest room next to his study. He went in with a Zola novel and undressed, but he couldn't concentrate on reading and so lay awake thinking. In his imagination his appendix took just the upturn he was hoping for. There was absorption, then evacuation, then the restoration of normal functioning. *Yes, it's really true!* he told himself. *You just have to help nature along.* He remembered his medicine, got up, took some, lay down on his back, and waited attentively for the drops to take their salutary effect and deaden the pain. *All I have to do is take them regularly and avoid harmful influences; even now I'm already feeling a little bit better, in fact much better.* He blew out the candle and laid on his side . . . His appendix was improving, it was absorbing. Suddenly he felt the familiar old pain, dully aching, persistent, silent, dreadful. In his mouth the same fetid taste. His heart sank, his mind was dazed. "O God, o my God," he moaned. "It's back, it's back, it'll never go away." And suddenly he saw everything from another perspective. *Appendix? Kidney?* he asked himself. *It's not about appendices and kidneys. This is a matter of life and... death. Yes, life was in me and now it's leaving, and I can't stop it. I can't. Why lie to myself? Isn't it obvious to everyone but me that I'm dying, that it's just a question of how many weeks, or days—it could come right now. Where there was light it's now covered in darkness. I was here, and now I'm headed . . . elsewhere! But where?* A chill came over him, his breathing stopped. The pounding of his heart was all he could hear.

If there's no me, what will there be? There'll be nothing. Where am I going to go, when I'm not anywhere? I mean— death, actual death? No, I don't want it! He leapt up to light a candle, rifled around with quivering hands, dropped a candlestick onto the floor with the candle still in it, and fell back down on his pillow. *What's the use? It makes no difference,* he said to himself, staring wide-eyed into the darkness. *Death. Yes. Death. And not one of them knows it, or wants to know; they don't even feel sorry for me. They're playing the piano.* Far off, from beyond the door, he heard a peal of voices and a ritornello. *It's all the same to them, and they'll get theirs, the fools. Mine may come sooner, but theirs is coming. Listen to how much fun they're having, the animals!* Rage was strangling him. He was consumed in burning, intolerable anguish. It couldn't be that everyone has always been doomed to this horrible fear. He got up.

Something's not right; I need to calm down, I need to rethink everything from the beginning. And so he began to reconsider. *Yes, the beginning of the illness. I bumped my side, and I was perfectly myself that day and the next; it hurt a little, and then a little more, then the doctors, then despondency and deepening melancholy, more doctors; meanwhile I was edging ever closer to the abyss. Less strength. Closer, closer. And now I've wasted away and there's no light in my eyes. Just death, and me thinking about my appendix. I keep thinking of how it's going to get better, but this is death. Can it really be death?* Horror descended upon him again, he felt as if he couldn't breathe, and bent down to grope for the matches with an elbow pressed against his nightstand. It was in his way and it hurt him, and he got mad at it, pressed against it even harder, and finally tumbled back onto the bed. Breathless, choked in despair, he rolled onto his back, thinking he would die at any second.

Meanwhile, the guests were leaving and Praskovya Fedorovna was seeing them off. She heard something fall and came in.

"What's wrong?"

"Nothing. Just an accident."

She went out and came back with a candle. He was laying there, panting for breath like a man who'd just run a verst, and he fixed his eyes on her.

"Jean, what is it?"

"Nothing . . . an accident . . ."

Why bother telling her? She won't understand, he thought.

And she really didn't understand. She lit his candle with hers and ran out to see another guest off.

When she came back, he was lying on his back, staring up.

"What's the matter with you? Are you feeling worse?"

"Yes."

She shook her head and took a seat. "You know, Jean, I'm thinking that maybe we'd better ask Leshchetitsky to come to the house."

She meant the famous doctor, and she must not have been worrying about money. He smiled malignantly and said, "No." She got up, walked over, and kissed him on the forehead.

He hated her from the depths of his soul whenever she kissed him like that, and it took an effort not to shove her away.

"Good night. Pray God you'll fall asleep."

"Yes."

Ivan Ilych could see he was dying, and was in unceasing despair.

In his heart he knew he was dying, but he not only couldn't get used to it, he simply couldn't grasp it, couldn't grasp it at all.

The example of syllogistic reasoning he had read in Kiezewetter's *Logic*—"Gaius is a man, men are mortal, therefore Gaius is mortal"—had always seemed to him true only in relation to Gaius, not to himself. That it was true of this man Gaius, and of men in general, made absolute sense; but he was no Gaius and was not some man in general. He had always had something unique about him that separated him from others—as little Vanya with his mama and papa, with Mitya and Volodya, with his toys, and his coachman and nanny, and later with Katyusha, with all the pleasures, sorrows, delights of childhood, adolescence, youth. What to Gaius was the striped leather ball that little Vanya had loved so much? What did Gaius have to do with him kissing his mother's hand, and had Gaius ever heard the silken rustle of his mother's dress? Had he rioted over the pirogies at the law school? Had this Gaius ever fallen in love? And could Gaius ever preside over a courtroom the way he did?

So of course, Gaius could be mortal, and it was right for him to die, but for me, little Vanya, for Ivan Ilych, with all my thoughts and emotions—for me it's a different story. It can't possibly be that *I* have to die. That would be too horrible.

That was how it felt to him.

If I had to die like Gaius, somewhere deep inside I'd know it, but I don't; and all my friends and I—we understood that for us it's different than for Gaius. And now here it is! he said to himself. *It can't be. It just can't be, but it is. How could it be true? How am I to supposed to understand such a thing?*

He could not understand it and tried to push it away as false, wrong, and morbid, and to replace it with other, proper and healthy thoughts. But not just the thought but the reality of it all kept coming back to stand before him.

And so he summoned other thoughts to replace this one, different ones in turn, hoping for something to lean on. He tried to return to the trains of thought that had occupied him before he'd become obsessed with death. But—strange thing, this—everything that had earlier obscured, hidden, obliterated his awareness of death, had now completely lost that function. Ivan Ilych came to spend the better part of his time trying to regain that ability. He said to himself, *I'll throw myself into my work—after all, it used to be all I lived for.* And so he went to court, blocking out all his doubts. He joined conversations with colleagues and sat, with his old, accustomed absentmindedness, giving the crowd a thoughtful once-over and resting his emaciated hands on the oak chair's armrests just as he always had, leaning in to whisper to a colleague, shuffling papers, and then suddenly lifting his eyes and straightening in his chair to pronounce the formula that opened proceedings. But in the middle of everything the pain in his side, paying no regard to the dignity of the proceedings, started up some noxious proceedings of its own. Ivan Ilych turned his attention to it and tried to push it away, but it soldiered on, It came and stood right before him, watching him, rooted to the spot, all flame and putridity, and he began to ask himself again, *Can It really be the only truth?* Both his colleagues and their subordinates would notice with surprise and dismay that he, once so brilliant and meticulous a judge, was growing confused and making mistakes. He shook himself, tried to get hold of himself and somehow conclude the session, and then went home with the sad awareness that work could not, as it had before, hide from him what he wanted hidden; that he couldn't get rid of It just by heading to court. And what was worst of all was that It was demanding his attention not to get him to do anything, but just so that he would look at It, look It right in the face, look at It and, without doing a thing, suffer inexpressible torment.

And so, trying to save himself from this state, Ivan Ilych looked for consolation, for other screens to block It out, and there were other screens that for a short time spared him, but they would always not so much collapse as prove transparent, as though It shone through everything and nothing could obscure It.

Sometimes then he would go into the drawing room he had furnished, the room where he had fallen—the room where, for the sake of its decoration (how toxically ludicrous it was for him to think about it now) he had offered up his life, for he knew that his illness had begun with the bruise. He would go in and see that something had scuffed the lacquered surface of the table there. Trying to figure out what, he would see it was the bronze ornamentation of an album that was bent at its edge. He would take up the expensive album that he had laid out with love, and grow annoyed at his daughter and her friends for their untidiness—something was torn off here, photographs were upside-down there. He would diligently put everything back in order, and bend the ornament back into shape.

Then he would think to move this whole *établissement* of albums to the other corner, nearer the flowers. He would call the footman, either his daughter or his wife might come to help; but everything would be all right, because he wasn't thinking about It; It was nowhere to be seen.

But whenever he moved things by himself his wife would say, "Calm down, let people help you, you'll hurt yourself again," and all at once It would shine through his screens, he would see It. It was blindingly bright, he still hoped It would darken, but he could not help thinking about his side—and there It would be sitting, aching just as ever, and he could not forget It, and It would stare him down from behind the flowers. What did anything else matter?

And I lost my life as if sailing into a storm, except right here, for this curtain. How horrible and how ridiculous! It can't be true! Can't be, but is.

He would go into his study, to lie down and be alone again with It, eye to eye with It, and do nothing there with It. Just look at It and grow cold.

VII   How it happened is impossible to say—because it happened step by step, imperceptibly—but in the third month of Ivan Ilych's illness his wife, and daughter, and his son also, the servants, his acquaintances, his doctors, and, most of all, he himself, came to realize that all the interest other people had in him was based solely on the fact that he would soon vacate his post at last, would free the living from the prison of his company, and would himself be freed of his suffering.

He slept less and less; he was given opium which began to be sprinkled with morphine. But things were not getting easier for him. The dulled, melancholy boredom of his semiconsciousness at first provided him the relief of something new, but it soon grew as torturous as, or more so than, the pain itself.

Special foods were prepared for him according to the instructions of doctors; but they were always blander and blander, and more and more revolting.

Special arrangements also had to be made for him to move his bowels, and this was crushing to him. Crushing for its uncleanness, its impropriety, and its odor, and from the knowledge that another person had to participate.

But even in this nastiest business there was one consolation for Ivan Ilych: Gerasim, the muzhik who helped out in the kitchen, always came by to see after him.

Gerasim was a clean, fresh-faced young peasant grown chubby on town food. Always cheerful, always bright. At first the sight of him, clean and dressed in impeccably Russian style, performing so disgusting a task, embarrassed Ivan Ilych.

One time, having got up from the toilet, and too weak to pull his trousers up, he tumbled into a soft armchair and with horror surveyed his enfeebled thighs, the muscles on them now starkly defined.

Gerasim came in with a strong, easy tread, giving off a pleasant scent of fresh winter air, wearing thick boots that still smelled of tar, a clean Hessian apron, and a clean printed shirt, its sleeves rolled up over powerful young arms, and, not looking at Ivan Ilych—apparently stifling the joy of being alive that radiated from his face—walked up to the chamber pot.

"Gerasim," Ivan Ilych said weakly.

Gerasim, startled, gave a shudder, obviously worried he had done something wrong, and in a quick motion turned his fresh, simple face, young and kind, from which a beard was just beginning to sprout, to the sick man.

"What would you like, sir?"

"I suppose you must find this unpleasant. Forgive me. I can't help it."

"Oh, why, sir," and Gerasim's eyes glistened and he flashed his young white teeth, "what's a little bit of trouble? The thing with you is that you're unwell, is all."

And he did his usual task with agile, strong hands and walked lightly out of the room. Five minutes later, stepping just as lightly, he came back.

Ivan Ilych was sunk into the armchair as before.

"Gerasim," he said, when he saw that the pot had been cleaned and replaced, "please help me, come here." Gerasim approached him. "Lift me up. It's too hard for me to do alone, and I've sent Dmitri away."

Gerasim approached him; he wrapped his strong arms around him just as nimbly as he had stepped out of the room before, lifted him up softly and held him there with one arm, while with the other he tightened Ivan Ilych's trousers and would have set him down. But Ivan Ilych asked to be helped to the sofa. Gerasim, without effort and without exerting any apparent pressure, led him, nearly carried him, to the sofa and eased him down.

"Thank you. How gracefully you do . . . well, everything."

Gerasim smiled again and turned to leave. But Ivan Ilych found his company so soothing that he did not want to dismiss him.

"Here, do me a favor: please bring that chair over. No, no, that one, here, put it under my legs. I feel better with my legs elevated."

Gerasim brought the chair, setting it down carefully in place and lifting his feet onto it; and it seemed to Ivan Ilych that the pain eased up on him as soon as Gerasim lifted his legs.

"It'd be better to have my legs higher still," Ivan Ilych said. "Hand me that pillow over there."

Gerasim did so. Again he lifted Ivan Ilych's legs and placed the pillow under them. Again things got better for Ivan Ilych while Gerasim was holding his legs up. And then when he lowered them, things seemed to worsen again.

"Gerasim," he said to him, "are you busy right now?"

"Not at all, sir," said Gerasim, who had in his time in town learned how to speak to a nobleman.

"What have you got left to do?"

"What have I got to do? Everything's already taken care of, except chopping wood for tomorrow."

"Then hold my legs up a little higher, could you?"

"Of course, sir, I'm glad to." Gerasim lifted his legs up, and it seemed to Ivan Ilych that in this position he felt no pain at all.

"But what about the firewood?"

"Don't you worry about that. We'll find time for it."

Ivan Ilych told Gerasim to sit holding his legs up and talk to him. And—strange to say—it seemed to him that he felt better while Gerasim was holding his legs.

From then on Ivan Ilych would sometimes call for Gerasim and have him hold his legs up on his shoulders, and he liked talking with him. Gerasim did this easily and willingly, and with a kindness that moved Ivan Ilych. Health, strength, vitality in all other people offended him; but somehow Gerasim's strength and vitality were not burdensome, they were soothing.

Ivan Ilych's coldest torment was the lie—known by everyone to be a lie—that he was merely sick, not dying, and that he needed only bedrest and treatment, and would be fine. Of course he knew that no matter what he did there would be no resolution for him except more miserable suffering and finally death. And this lie tormented him, it tormented him that everyone refused to admit what they all knew and he knew, that they preferred to lie about his terrible situation, and that they forced him to take part in the lie himself. This deception, this dishonesty, this lie, imposed on him on the very eve of his death, reduced the dreadful, solemn act of his own death to the level of all their visits, their curtains, their sturgeon dinners . . . it was ungodly torture for him. And—strangely—many times while they were performing this charade around him, he had nearly cried out: *Stop lying already! Stop deceiving me! You know and I know that I'm dying, so at the very least stop lying about it!* But he had never had the heart to do it. The dreadful, horrible act of his dying had been reduced, he now saw, in the lives of all the people around him to the level of a passing discomfort, something that was mildly distasteful (as though they were walking into a drawing room that had a nasty smell about it), it was all done in accordance to the same code of *propriety* that he had served his entire life; he saw that no one would feel sorry for him because no one wanted to fully comprehend his situation. Gerasim was the only one who showed any sympathy. And so it was only around Gerasim that Ivan Ilych ever felt at ease. He felt good when Gerasim held his legs up, sometimes the whole night through without a rest, not bothering to sleep, saying, "Don't you trouble yourself over it, Ivan Ilych, I'll get some rest later," or when suddenly, speaking to him for the first time in the informal, he added, "I mean, it'd be one thing if you weren't so sick—but why shouldn't I help you out now?" Gerasim was the only one who did not lie; he seemed to be the only one who understood what was going on and thought it pointless to hide the facts, who simply took pity on his emaciated, vanishing master. Once when Ivan Ilych was sending him away he even said it outright:

"We all die in our time. Why I should begrudge you a little sweat?" Of course what he was saying was that his sweat represented no burden, because it was spent on a dying man, just as he hoped that someone would sweat a little for him when his time came.

Apart from the lying, or maybe on account of it, the greatest of Ivan Ilych's torments was that nobody offered the kind of sympathy he wanted: at certain moments, after prolonged suffering, what Ivan Ilych wanted most, though he would have been ashamed to admit it, was for somebody to feel sorry for him as if he were a sick little boy. He wanted to be caressed, kissed, cried over as children are caressed and comforted. He knew that he was an important jurist, that he had a graying beard, and so this was impossible; all the same it was what he wanted. And in his relationship with Gerasim he found something approaching it, and so his relationship with Gerasim gave him comfort. Ivan Ilych longed to cry, longed to be caressed and cried over, and here comes his colleague Justice Shebek, and instead of weeping and being caressed Ivan Ilych puts on a somber, stern, weighty air and out of utter inertia starts blurting out his opinion on the Court of Cassation's recent decision, insisting doggedly on it, in fact. This lie that was all around and in fact inside of him poisoned, worse than anything, the last days in the life of Ivan Ilych.

VIII It was morning. It had to be morning, since Gerasim had left and the footman Pyotr had come in, put out the candles, opened one of the curtains, and begun cleaning up at the pace of a snail. Whether it was morning or evening, Friday or Sunday, made no difference, it was all the same: that gnawing, torturous pain that never relented for a second; the awareness of life inexorably departing but not yet departed; the same death approaching, hateful and terrifying, the only reality and yet an utter deception. What, in the face of it all, were days, weeks, hours?

"Wouldn't you like some tea, sir?"

He needs the orderliness of seeing a nobleman take his tea in the morning, he thought, and said only:

"No."

"Wouldn't it be more comfortable, sir, over on the sofa?"

He needs to put the room in order, and I'm in the way—I'm dirt, disarray, he thought, and said only:

"No, leave me alone."

The footman stayed around, tinkering. Ivan Ilych stretched out his arm. Pyotr approached him obligingly.

"What is it, sir?"

"My watch."

Pyotr picked up the watch, which was within Ivan Ilych's reach, and gave it to him.

"It's half past nine. They're not up yet?"

"They aren't, sir, no. Except Vasiliy Ivanovich"—this was his son—"who has already left for school, and Praskovya Fedorovna, who told me to wake her if you asked. Shall I?"

"No, don't." *Should I have some tea?* he wondered. "Yes, some tea . . . bring it to me."

Pyotr headed to the doorway. But it had become terrifying for Ivan Ilych to be left alone anywhere. *How can I keep him here? That's it: my medicine.* "Pyotr, bring me my drops." *Who knows, maybe the medicine will even help.* He took a spoonful, gulped it down. *No, it's not going to help. It's all nonsense, trickery*, he decided as soon as that sickening, familiar, hopeless taste filled his mouth. *No, I can't let myself believe it. But what pain, what pain, if only it would let up for just a minute.* And he groaned. Pyotr came back. "No, go ahead, bring me my tea."

Pyotr left. Ivan Ilych, alone, let out a moan, not so much from the pain (which is not to say it was not horrible) as from his plodding, slow despair. *All the same, always the same, these endless days and nights. If only it would be quicker. Ah, quicker? If only* what *would come quicker? Death, oblivion. No, no! Anything is better than that!*

When Pyotr had come back with a tray of tea, Ivan Ilych looked at it him for a long time with a perplexed stare, not understanding who or what he was. Pyotr's embarrassment brought Ivan Ilych back to his senses.

"Yes," he said, "my tea. Good, put it down. Just help me wash up and put on a clean shirt."

And Ivan Ilych began washing. He washed his face and hands, pausing when he needed rest, scrubbed his teeth and brushed his hair, then looked in the mirror. He suddenly felt terrified, especially by the sight of the hair laying flat across his ashen forehead.

Knowing that the sight of his body would be even more frightening, he did not look at himself while he changed his shirt. And finally it was all done. He put on his dressing-gown, wrapped himself in a plaid rug and eased into his armchair for some tea. For a minute he felt refreshed, but, as soon as he took his first sip, that same taste, that same pain. He guzzled it quickly and lay down, stretching his legs out, and dismissed Pyotr.

It was all the same. A flicker of hope drowned by a raging sea of despair, and always that pain, that pain, the crushing, blank melancholy always the same. When he was alone he felt that melancholy terribly and would want to call for somebody, but he knew that in the company of others it would be even worse. *If only I could get a little more morphine—that would take my mind off it.*

I'll tell that doctor that he needs to think up something new. I can't possibly go on like this, it's impossible.

An hour goes by like that, then two. But then there is a ring at the front door. Could be the doctor. In fact it is the doctor, fresh and full of life, fat and cheerful, with that same look on his face that seems to say, *And here you were starting to get frightened! Well, we'll have you fixed up.* The doctor knows that the look is not quite suited to this situation, but he's already put it on his face and cannot undo it, like a person making social calls in a frock coat he's been wearing since the morning. The doctor rubs his hands together vigorously, consolingly.

"I'm cold. A nasty little chill out there. Just let me warm myself up," he says with that same expression, as though all he had to do was wait until he had got warm, and then he would fix everything right up.

"Well, then. How are you feeling?"

Ivan Ilych senses that the doctor would rather ask, *So how's that little problem of yours?*, but even he knows better, and so he says, "How did your night go?"

Ivan Ilych shoots the doctor a look as if to say, *Oh, come on already—aren't you ever ashamed of hiding the truth?*

But the doctor does not want to understand this question.

And Ivan Ilych says:

"Wretched, just completely wretched. The pain never ceases, it never leaves me. If only you had something for me to take!"

"Yes, yes, you sick people, you're all the same, always talking that way. Well, I'm warm enough now. Even Praskovya Fedorovna—that most demanding woman—could not possibly object to my temperature. Okay, now: Hello." And the doctor shakes his hand.

And, casting off his playfulness, the doctor assumes a more serious face to begin an examination of the patient, taking his pulse and temperature, and beginning to tap around and listen.

Ivan Ilych knows for a certainty that this is all pretense and empty gesture, but when the doctor gets down on his knees and stretches out over him, brings his ear first higher then lower, and then with the most meaning-laden look on his face makes all kinds of gymnastic contortions over him, Ivan Ilych is persuaded by it, just as he used to be persuaded by the arguments of lawyers whom he knew perfectly well were lying, and whose reasons for lying were no secret.

The doctor, kneeling into the sofa, is still tapping at something when Praskovya Fedorovna's silk dress rustles at the doorway and she is heard reprimanding Pyotr for not telling her the doctor has come by.

She comes in, kisses her husband, and right away starts trying to demonstrate that she has been up for a long time and it is only through a misunderstanding that she did not greet the doctor on his arrival.

Ivan Ilych looks at her, studies her from head to toe, and adds her fairness, her plumpness, and the smoothness of her arms and neck to his charges against her, then adds the luster of her hair and the twinkle in her eyes. He loathes her with all the powers of his heart, and at her touch he is smacked by a gush of surging hatred.

Her attitude toward him and his illness has not changed. Just as the doctor had cultivated in himself an attitude toward his patients that he could no longer change, so too had she cultivated an attitude toward him—that he has always failed to do something he was supposed to do, and has no one to blame but himself, and she is reproaching him only lovingly—and there is nothing she can do now to change this attitude.

"Oh, just look at him, doesn't do a thing he's told! He doesn't take his medicine when he's supposed to. And worst of all, he lays around in a position that's probably bad for him—with his legs up."

She told the whole story of how he would force Gerasim to hold his legs up.

The doctor smiled with a condescending tenderness that seemed to say, *Well, you know, these people—these sick people—they sometimes think up little absurdities like that; but we must forgive them.*

When the examination was over, the doctor looked at his watch, and then Praskovya Fedorovna announced to Ivan Ilych that, as he had requested, she had invited the famous doctor, and that he and Mikhail Danilovich (the regular doctor) would examine him together and discuss their findings.

"Just please don't try to argue with me. I'm doing this for myself," she said ironically, trying to make him feel that she did everything for him and had said it this way just so he would not be able to refuse. He glowered and said nothing. He felt that the deception that was surrounding him had got so confused that it was hard to really figure anything out.

As far as he was concerned, everything she did was purely for herself, and now she was telling him that she was doing for herself just what she *was* doing for herself, as though it were so incredible a thing that he had no choice but to believe the opposite.

Sure enough, the famous doctor showed up at half past eleven. There were all the listenings, just as before, and earnest conversations with him and in the other room about his kidney and appendix, questions and answers with such an air of significance that instead of the real question of life and death that now alone confronted him the question they ended up discussing concerned the kidney and appendix that had somehow gone astray, and which Mikhail Danilovich and the celebrity were now going to attack and force to right themselves.

The famous doctor took leave of him with a serious but not quite hopeless look. And to the timid question that Ivan Ilych put to him, his shimmering eyes raised in fear and hope, as to whether there was any chance of recovery, he answered that he could not make any guarantees but the possibility did exist. The look of hope that Ivan Ilych flashed the doctor was so pitiful that, having seen it, even Praskovya Fedorovna broke into tears as she crossed through the doors to the study to hand the famous doctor his fee.

The boost that the doctor's reassurance had given him did not keep up for long. Again that same room, those same pictures, curtains, wallpaper, bottles, and that same aching, suffering body. And Ivan Ilych began to moan; he was given an injection, and he was forgotten about.

When he woke up night had begun to fall; dinner was brought to him. He ate his broth with some difficulty; and again it was all the same, and again the night was encroaching.

After dinner, at seven o'clock, Praskovya Fedorovna came into his room in evening wear, with fat, corseted breasts and traces of powder on her face. She had reminded him that morning that they had theater tickets. Sarah Bernhardt was in town, and they had a box, which he had insisted on their buying. By now he had forgotten all about it, and her orders insulted him. But he concealed his offense when he remembered that it had been he himself who had insisted on getting the box, because the aesthetic pleasure would prove educational for the children.

Praskovya Fedorovna walked in looking self-satisfied, but also as though feeling guilty about something. She sat down, asked how he was feeling—though only, as he could tell, for the sake of asking, and not to find anything out, knowing perfectly well that there was nothing to find out—and then went about saying what she had to say: that she would not have gone no matter what, but the box had been taken, and Ellen and her daughter were going, as well as Petrishchev (the examining magistrate engaged to their daughter), and they could not be allowed to go alone, but she would have preferred to sit with him for a while, and he had better take care of himself and follow the doctor's instructions while she was gone.

"Yes, and Fyodor Petrovich (the fiancé) would like to come in. Is that all right? Liza too."

"Let them in."

His daughter came in in her evening clothes, her young body exposed, a body that was—while his body forced him to suffer so—strong, healthy, clearly in love, and indignant at the illness, misery, and death disrupting her happiness.

In too came Fyodor Petrovich in a frock-coat, his hair curled *à la Capoul*, with his long sinewy neck penned in by a stiff white collar, the white breast of his shirt seeming massive, and his strong thighs in tightly fitted black trousers, with one hand gloved tightly in white and holding an opera hat.

Behind him his schoolboy son crept in wearing his new uniform, the poor little thing, in gloves and with those blue circles under his eyes whose significance Ivan Ilych knew all too well.

His son had always seemed pathetic to him. And now the boy's frightened look of pity was dreadful to see. Except for Gerasim, it seemed to Ivan Ilych that Vasya was the only one who understood and felt sorry for him.

Everybody sat down, and he was again asked about his health. A silence fell. Liza asked her mother about the opera glasses. A little quarrel broke out between mother and daughter over who had put them where. It was quite unpleasant.

Fyodor Petrovich asked Ivan Ilych whether he had ever seen Sarah Bernhardt. At first Ivan Ilych did not understand what was being asked, and then said:

"No, have you?"

"Yes, in *Adrienne Lecouvreur.*"

Praskovya Fedorovna said that she had been especially good in that. Her daughter disagreed. A conversation began about the grace and realism of her acting—that very same conversation that always comes up, and is always the same.

In the middle of the conversation Fyodor Petrovich glanced at Ivan Ilych and broke off what he was saying. The others looked and fell likewise silent. Ivan Ilych was staring with radiant eyes straight ahead, clearly furious with them. Someone needed to make the situation better again, but there was just no way to do it. Someone needed to disrupt the silence with something. But no one had it in them, and they became frightened that the feigned propriety would shatter and the truth become plain to all. Liza was the first to gather the courage to break the silence. She wanted to conceal what they were all going through, but instead she just blurted out.

"Well, if we are going, it's time," she said, having glanced at her watch, a gift from her father, and with a barely discernable smile of mysterious significance to her fiancé, stood up and rustled her dress.

Everyone stood up, excused themselves, and left.

When they had gone, Ivan Ilych could have sworn he felt better: there was no deception—it had gone out with them—though the pain remained. That unrelenting pain, that unrelenting terror made nothing any harder, nothing any easier. And things were worse all the time.

Again minute followed minute, hour followed hour, all exactly the same, with no cessation, and making all the more terrible the inevitable ending.

"Yes, send for Gerasim," he said, answering Pyotr's question.

It was late at night when his wife got back. She came in on tiptoes, but he heard her: he opened his eyes and then shut them again in a hurry. She wanted to send Gerasim away and sit alone with him. He opened his eyes and said:

"No. Go."

"Are you suffering much?"

"What's the difference."

"Take some opium."

He assented and drank a dose. She left.

Until three in the morning he lay in a tormented oblivion. It seemed to him that he had been pushed, along with his pain, into a black bag, deep and narrow, was being pushed all the time, ever deeper, by a force that could never be satisfied. And everywhere this state, horrible to him, was rounded out in suffering. Though he was afraid, he wanted in the same breath to give out; he struggled against but also abetted it. Then all of a sudden he broke through the bottom of the sack and plunged, and then came to. And there was Gerasim, sitting faithfully at the foot of the bed, dozing peacefully, patiently, while he was laying with his gaunt legs in their stockings on Gerasim's shoulders; the same candle with its shade was there, as was the same pain never ceasing.

"Go away, Gerasim," he whispered.

"I don't mind. I'll just sit here."

"No. Go away."

He removed his legs from Gerasim's shoulders, turned sidewise on his arms, and began feeling sorry for himself. He waited until Gerasim had gone into the next room, and then lost all his restraint and started bawling like a child. He cried for his helplessness, his terrible solitude, for the cruelty of man, the cruelty of God, for God's absence. *What have you done this for? Why have you brought me to this? For what, for what are you torturing me so horribly?* He did not expect an answer, he cried for the fact that there was not and would never be an answer. The pain welled up again, but he did not stir, called to no one. He said to himself: *Well all right, so smite me! But for what? What did I ever do to you, that I should be punished like this?*

After a while he quieted down, not only ceased crying but halted his breath and became all attention: as though he were listening not to a voice speaking in sounds but to the voice of his heart, to a trail of thought wafting up inside him.

What is it that you need? was the first clear, articulated thought that he heard. *What is it that you need? What is it that you need?* he repeated to himself. *What? Not to suffer. To live,* he answered.

And again he poured himself into such attention that even his pain did not distract him.

Live? Live how? the voice in his heart asked.

To live, of course, how I used to: happily, and well.

How you lived, happily and well? the voice asked. And in his imagination he began going over the best moments of his life. But—strange thing—all these glad moments seemed quite different now from how they had registered at the time. All of them, that is, except for the earliest recollections of his childhood. There, in childhood, there had been something so transcendently pleasant that if it would only return he could carry on living. But the person who had lived through all these pleasures no longer existed: it was as though he were reminiscing about some old friend.

As soon as he got to the period which resulted in the present Ivan Ilych, everything that had seemed at the time a pleasure now turned before his eyes into something meager, even disgusting.

The further from childhood and the closer to the present, the more trivial and dubious the pleasures became. It began with law school. There had been something profoundly good there: he had known high spirits, had known friendship, hope. But by his upperclassman years the good times had grown scant. Later, in his first job at the governor's office, he again had had some good times: there were memories of his love for a woman. With time it had all got confused, and there was less good in his life still. And further on there had been still less good than that, and the later on in life, the less.

His marriage . . . so accidental, and such a disappointment, with his wife's bad breath, and her sensuality, and their hypocrisy! His moribund professional life, the obsession with money, it had built up over a year, and then two, then ten, twenty—and always the same. The further on in years, the more deadening it became. *In perfectly measured steps I went downhill imagining it was up. That's just how it was. In public opinion I was on my way up, and the whole time my life was slipping away from under me . . . and now it's all over with, and it's time to die!*

All right, but what is it all for? It can't be that life was so meaningless, repugnant. And if it really was this repugnant and meaningless, then why die, and die suffering? Something's wrong.

Maybe I didn't live as I should've? the thought leapt to his mind. *But how could that be, when I did everything as I was supposed to,* he wondered, before promptly dismissing this only solution to the riddle of life and death as something absolutely impossible.

Well, what do you want now? To live? Live how? To live as you live in the courtroom when the bailiff shouts, "Court is in session! Court is in session! Order in the court!" he repeated to himself. *And here is my judgment! But I'm not guilty!* he screamed with wrath. *For what?* And he began again to weep and, after turning toward the wall, started to pore over just one question: what was the point of all this horror?

But no matter how much he thought about it he could not find an answer. And when the thought came to him, as it would often come, that it was all happening because he had not lived right, he immediately recollected all the correctness of his life and forced the strange thought away.

X Two more weeks went by. Ivan Ilych could no longer get up from the sofa. He did not want to lay in bed and so he lay on the sofa. And so, laying nearly all the time with his face to the wall, he endured in solitude all his unresolving torments and brooded over the same unresolving question. *What is this? Don't I know this is death?* And an inner voice answered: *Yes, you know it.*

Why all these tortures? And the voice answered: *Not for any reason.* There was nothing beside this, nothing beyond it.

Since the very beginning of his illness, ever since the first time he had gone to the doctor, his life had been divided into two moods that came over him in turns: first despair and the expectation of an incomprehensible and awful death; then hopefulness and a keen fascination with all the workings of his body. First he would imagine nothing but a kidney or an appendix that had for a time deserted its post; then nothing but incomprehensible and terrible death, from which there could be no possible means of deliverance.

These two moods had been alternating one with the other since the very start of his illness, but the further his condition progressed the more dubious and fantastic his thoughts about his liver became, and the more real too his sense of impending death.

He had only to remember what he had been three months ago, and see what he was now, to realize how steadily he had been going downhill, for any possibility of hope to be shattered.

Lately in that loneliness in which he found himself, laying with his face to the back of the sofa, that loneliness in the middle of a bustling town, among his many friends and his family—that loneliness more profound than could be found anywhere, any spot on the seafloor, or any stretch of land—in these late days of horrific loneliness Ivan Ilych lived only by his memories of the past. One after another he imagined scenes from his life. He would always begin with the most recent and proceed to the earliest, to his childhood, and settle there. If he thought of the stewed prunes he had been offered for dinner today he would instantly begin reminiscing about the wrinkled French plums of his childhood, about their special taste and the way his mouth watered when he got to the pit, and right alongside memories of this taste was a rush of other memories: his nanny, his brother, his toys. *No no, not this—it's too painful,* Ivan Ilych would say to himself and he forced himself back to the present again. The button on the back of the sofa and the wrinkles in the morocco. *Morocco's expensive and wears easily; we quarreled because of it. But there was a different morocco, and a different quarrel, when we tore father's portfolio and he punished us, and mama brought us tarts.* And again it all stopped on his childhood, and again it was too painful for Ivan Ilych, and he tried to think of something to else to get his mind off it.

And now again, with this train of memories, another made its path through his heart—of how his illness had taken hold and developed. Just as before, the further back he looked, the more life there had been in him; both the more sweetness to life, and the more of life itself. And the two tendencies had become firmly intertwined. *As my tortures have grown worse and worse, so has my life grown worse and worse,* he thought. There had been one point of light far back at the start of everything, and ever since everything had gotten blacker and blacker, and moved quicker and quicker. *In inverse proportion to the distance from death squared,* Ivan Ilych thought. And this image of a stone plummeting and picking up speed sunk deep into his heart. Life, that series of increasing torments, flies faster and faster as it nears its end, the most terrifying suffering of all. *I'm flying . . .* He shuddered, repositioned himself, wanted to resist; but he already knew that resistance was futile, and again with eyes exhausted by vision but unable not to look at what was in front of them he looked at the back of the sofa and waited—waited for that horrible plunge, the shock, the extinguishment. *It's impossible to resist it*, he said to himself. *If only I could understand what this is all for! But that's impossible too. I could explain it all if I hadn't lived as meticulously as I should have. But there's no way of comprehending this*, he said to himself, thinking of all the rules, proprieties, and decencies of his life. *There's really no way I can admit to that*, he said, drawing his lips into a smile as though anyone might see him and be deceived. *There is no explanation! Torture, death . . . for what?*

XI Two weeks went by like that. During that time, something happened that Ivan Ilych and his wife had been wishing for: Petrishchev made a formal proposal. It happened in the evening. The next day Praskovya Fedorovna came into her husband's room, chewing over the best way to relate the news, but that very night Ivan Ilych had taken a serious turn for the worse. Praskovya Fedorovna found him on the sofa same as ever, but in a different position than usual. He was laying on his back, groaning and staring ahead with glassy eyes.

She started talking about his medications. He turned his eyes to her. She did not manage to finish what she had started saying: such was the rage articulated in his glare, and directed precisely at her. "For Christ's sake, let me die in peace," he said.

She wanted to leave, but at that moment their daughter came in and walked over to say hello. He shot his daughter the same look he had given his wife, and to her questions about his health answered dryly that he would soon free them all from himself. Both women fell silent, sat around a while longer, and then left.

"What did we do?" Liza asked her mother. "You'd think it was all our fault! I feel bad for Papa, but what does he have to torture us for?"

The doctor showed up at his usual time. Ivan Ilych said to him, "Maybe . . ." maintaining his embittered gaze, then finally said:

"Come on, you know nothing can help me—leave me alone."

"We can ease your sufferings," the doctor said.

"No, you can't even manage that; leave me alone."

The doctor left for the drawing room and informed Praskovya Fedorovna that things were extremely bad, and there was only one option: opium could ease his suffering, which were his greatest torment.

The doctor declared that his physical sufferings were terrible, and he was right; but more horrible even than his physical sufferings were his moral sufferings, his greatest torment.

His moral sufferings were due to the fact that that night, as he had gazed at Gerasim's drowsy, kindhearted face with its prominent cheekbones, the question had suddenly come into his head: *What if my whole life, my entire conscious life, has been "false"?*

It occurred to him that what he had taken for a perfect impossibility—that he had not lived his life as one should—might in fact be the truth. It occurred to him that those scarcely detected impulses to struggle against what the people of highest social rank considered good, those feeble tendencies that he barely noticed and immediately suppressed, might in fact be what was real, and everything else what was false. His career, all the arrangements of his life and his family, his social and professional ambitions—each of them might be false. He tried to defend it all to himself, and suddenly the weakness of what he was defending became palpable to him. There was nothing, nothing to defend.

But if this is so, he said to himself, *and I'm leaving the world knowing I've ruined everything I was given, and there's no way to set it right—well, then what?* He laid on his back and began to go over his entire life from a totally new perspective. When in the morning he saw the footman, and later his wife, and later his daughter, and later the doctor, every step they took, every word they spoke confirmed the horrible revelation that had been laid bare to him the night before. In them he saw himself and everything he had lived by, and saw clearly that it was all false, all of it a monstrous and immense deceit foreclosing both life and death. The realization amplified his sufferings tenfold. He groaned and tossed and tore at his bedclothes. It seemed to him that they were choking and chafing him, and he hated them for it.

He was given a large dose of opium and he lost consciousness; but his agony started up again during dinner. He drove everyone away and began tossing from side to side.

His wife came into the room and said:

"Jean, darling, just do this for me." For me? "It can't hurt, and a lot of the time it helps. Come on, it's nothing. A lot of the time, even perfectly healthy people . . ."

He opened his eyes wide.

"What do you want me to do—take the sacrament? What for? There's no need! Except . . ."

She broke down crying.

"Yes, dear? I'll call for our priest, he's such a dear."

"Oh, very well," he muttered.

When the priest had come and heard his confession, he softened and felt as though his doubts, and along with them his sufferings, had been eased, and a moment of hope found its way to him. He started thinking again about his appendix and the possibility of setting it right. He took the sacrament with tears in his eyes.

When he lay down again after communion, he felt a moment's ease, and again a hope of recovery arose in him. He began thinking about the operation he had been offered. *To live, I want to live*, he told himself. His wife came in to congratulate him, and after the usual formula she added:

"Well, come on now, don't you feel better?"

Without looking at her, he muttered: "Yes."

Her clothes, her figure, the expression on her face, the sound of her voice—everything sang to him in unison: *False. Everything by which you have lived and live now is all a deception, a lie, concealing both life and death from you.* And as soon as he had the thought, hatred welled up within' him, a hatred accompanied by the most agonizing physical pain, themselves accompanied by an awareness of close, inescapable death. Something new started: it began to grind, and shoot, and to constrict his breath.

The look on his face when he said *Yes* had been horrible. Having forced it out, looking her square in the face, he turned onto his back, extraordinarily quickly considering his weakness, and cried out:

"Go away, go away, leave me alone!"

At that moment began three days of incessant screaming so terrible that two rooms away they couldn't be heard without horror. In the minute that he had answered his wife, he had immediately understood that he was gone, there was no turning back, the end had come, the very end, and his doubts were left unresolved, left to remain dangling in uncertainty.

"O! O! O!" he shouted in varying intonations. He started shouting, "I don't want to!" and then went back to his shrieking variations on the letter *o*.

All three days, which for him were no longer a measure of time, he flailed helplessly in that black bag into which he was now thrust by an invisible, overwhelming force. He fought as a prisoner sentenced to death fights the executioner, knowing that he cannot prevail; and with each minute he felt, despite all the efforts of his struggle, that he was getting closer and closer to what terrified him. It seemed that his torture consisted in being consigned to this black hole, and, even worse, in not being able to worm his way through it. The knowledge that life had been good prevented his wriggling through. And this justification of his struggle clung to him and held him back and tormented him worse than anything.

Suddenly an unknown force crushed against his chest, into his side, and a still stronger force constricted his breathing, he plunged down into the hole, and there, at the bottom, something was shining. What happened to him was like what happens sometimes in railcars, when you think you are going forward but are actually going backward, and suddenly realize your direction.

Yes, everything's been wrong, he told himself, *but it doesn't matter. One might do what's "right." But what* is *"right"?* he asked himself, and suddenly gained some calm.

It was the end of the third day, an hour before he would die. At just that moment his schoolboy son crept silently up to his father's bed. The dying man was shouting in despair and flailing his arms. His hand hit his son on the head; the boy grabbed the hand and, pressing it to his lips, exploded into tears.

This was the very moment that Ivan Ilych had fallen through, caught sight of the light, and had it revealed to him that his life might not have been what it should have, but there was still time to make up for it.

He asked himself what "right" really was and quieted down, taking in all the sounds he could. Suddenly he felt that someone was kissing his hand. He opened his eyes and caught sight of his little boy. He felt sorry for him. His wife came up to him. He looked at her. She was looking down at him with her mouth open, undried tears running down her nose and cheeks. He felt sorry for her.

Yes, I'm torturing them, he thought. *It's hard on them, but things'll be better after I die.* He wanted to tell them so, but could not marshal the strength to speak. *Anyhow, what's the point in talking, one must act,* he thought. With a twist of his eyes he pointed out the boy to his wife and said:

"Go . . . it's too much . . . for you too. . . ." He wanted to add Forgive me, but he said, "Forego me," and, without the strength to correct himself, waved his arm, knowing that the one who needed to understand it would.

And suddenly it became clear to him that what had been afflicting him and unabated was suddenly dissipating at once, and on both sides, on ten sides, on all sides. He felt sorry for them, he had to do something so things would not be too hard on them. To release them and liberate himself from all these sufferings. *How good, and how simple,* he thought. *And the pain? Where has it gone? Well, come on now—pain, where are you?*

He started to listen very closely for it.

Yes, yes, there it is. Well, what are you waiting for, pain, get going!

And my death? Where's that?

He searched for the fear of death he had grown used to but could not find it. Where was it? What death? He was without any kind of fear because death was nowhere near him.

Instead of death there was light.

"So that's what it is!" he suddenly uttered aloud. *What gladness!*

For him this all happened in a single instant, an instant whose meaning was no longer in flux. For the people assembled his agony would go on for another two hours. In his breast something rattled; a wheeze passed through his haggard body. In time the rattling and the wheezing grew less and less frequent.

"It's the end!" somebody said above him.

He heard these words and began repeating them in his heart. *It's the end of my death*, he said to himself. *There won't be anything else.*

He pulled in a breath, stopped halfway through it, straightened himself out, and died.

THE CONTEMPORARY ART OF THE NOVELLA

melville house classics

THE ART OF THE NOVELLA